The Secret Room

by

Hazel Townson

Illustrated by Martin Salisbury

You do not need to read this page – just get on with the book!

First published in Great Britain in 2000 by Barrington Stoke Ltd, Sandeman House, Trunk's Close, 55 High Street, Edinburgh EH1 1SR
www.barringtonstoke.co.uk

This edition published 2001

Reprinted 2002, 2003, 2005 (twice)

ISBN 1-902260-68-6

Printed in Great Britain by Bell & Bain Ltd

Meet The Author - Hazel Townson

What is your favourite animal?
A dog
What is your favourite boy's name?
Christopher
What is your favourite girl's name?
Catherine
What is your favourite food?
Strawberries
What is your favourite music?
Classical, especially Mahler
What is your favourite hobby?
Table tennis

Meet The Illustrator - Martin Salisbury

What is your favourite animal?
Any wild cat
What is your favourite boy's name?
Charles
What is your favourite girl's name?
Stella
What is your favourite food?
Sausages and mash
What is your favourite music?
Patsy Cline
What is your favourite hobby?
Collecting illustrated books

For my super son-in-law
Stuart Atherden

Contents

Chapter 1
The Iron Key

Adam Belman was bored. He had just changed schools in the middle of term and found the work here at Hope School far less interesting. There was too much teacher-talk and not enough action.

Besides, right now they were learning about the Second World War, a subject he found more boring than most. He was actually half-asleep in the middle of the lesson. His mind was drifting lazily along to nowhere when it suddenly snagged on something and jerked him awake. He might just have solved the first clue in a mystery!

Jade Green was the only one of his classmates who had shown any interest in him. She had hinted that the school possessed a secret room, though no one had ever been able to find it.

In the absence of anything better to do, Adam had spent his spare time wandering round the school building in search of some hollow wall or hidden door. Maybe if he found the secret room it would impress the others and gain him some friends.

Unfortunately, he hadn't picked up a single clue ... until now, in the middle of this boring lesson, when an exciting possibility occurred to him.

The teacher, Mr Evans, had laid down on his table a huge, old-fashioned iron key. The label hung over the table edge directly in front of Adam and read Stock Cupboard. The sight of that label now suggested a new angle on the mystery. For surely no stock cupboard ever needed a key so old or heavy? And especially in a school which had just been modernised? That label must be a cover-up for something far more sinister – like a secret room!

In an instant, Adam Belman was transformed, his brain working overtime. He must get hold of that key and begin to investigate at once.

By the end of the lesson Adam had shown so little interest in the Second World War that Mr Evans asked him to wait behind. This was Adam's great chance. He pretended to be confused and in need of help so he leaned eagerly across the teacher's table, managing to slip the key into his pocket.

That day a staff meeting had been arranged for half past three, directly after the final bell. What better opportunity to try out the key whilst the teachers were busy? The worst that could happen was that Mrs Yates the caretaker would spot him. In that case he would claim he'd been sent to look for his missing PE outfit and didn't dare go home without it.

Adam hid himself in the lavatories until quarter to four. Then he sneaked past the staffroom to make sure that the meeting had begun. Yes, he could hear voices talking and arguing and some chinking crockery. He also noticed that generous amounts of cigarette smoke were already curling under the staffroom door.

Satisfied, Adam made his way straight along to the stock cupboard, which he knew was in a dark corner off the main hall. This end of the hall had a dusty, brown curtain in front of it, behind which were stored the folding dinner tables, musical instruments, football gear and PE apparatus. In fact it was quite a scramble to reach the cupboard in the first place.

There was a huge keyhole set high in the cupboard door, into which his clumsy iron key fitted perfectly. With a quick check over his shoulder to make sure nobody was

THE STYLE OF MONET

watching, Adam finally turned the key and opened the door. At once a light came on inside the cupboard and he walked straight in.

As expected, he was faced with shelves of stationery, neatly piled notebooks and class sets of readers, sheet music, tissues and rulers and bundles of biros in boxes. Not a mystery in sight! No sign of any other door, no secret panel or sliding shelf. How disappointing!

Ah, well! It had been worth a try. Perhaps he'd hang on to the key for a while and see if it fitted anywhere else.

He was just about to turn and go when the door slammed shut behind him, switching off the light. Then a key turned in the outside lock. Mrs Yates must have seen the door was open and locked it with her own key. What a good thing Adam hadn't left his key in the door but still held it safe in his hand! No need to panic. Adam waited a moment to give Mrs Yates time to move away. Then, groping in the dark, he managed to find the keyhole and reopen the door. Now he did panic. A massive shock awaited him.

Gone was all the clutter which had lain behind the dusty, brown curtain. In fact, the curtain was also gone. Year 6's impressive art display In the Style of Monet, which up till then had covered three sides of the hall, was also gone. All that now remained on the walls were a couple of strange, old-fashioned posters – one saying 'Dig for Victory' and the other, 'Careless Talk Costs Lives'.

As Adam stared in amazement he began to notice other changes. Every window now had thick, black curtains instead of pretty, flowery ones and each pane of glass was

criss-crossed with strips of brown sticky-tape.

It was unthinkable that anyone, especially elderly Mrs Yates, could have made all these changes in that short space of time. Something very strange was happening – something very scary.

Had he discovered the secret room after all?

Chapter 2
A Siren Sounds

Adam stood rooted to the spot, unable to decide what to do. Should he step back into the cupboard at once and hope to regain reality? Or should he take courage and explore this weird and puzzling place which was basically the same as the school hall, yet amazingly different? It was a chance of a lifetime and would certainly provide him with a stunning tale to tell.

Instead of being half-ignored he'd be the centre of attention.

Before he could make up his mind a girl ran into the hall, saw him and called out, "Hurry up! The siren's gone! Didn't you hear it?"

To his great relief he saw that the girl was Jade Green. She was dashing off somewhere at great speed, clutching a coat and a cardboard box. For some strange reason, Jade had changed out of her school uniform into a shabby dress and cardigan which looked as if they had come from a charity shop.

Adam hadn't heard any siren. Feeling bewildered, he thought it was the fire alarm. Jade grabbed his arm and dragged him off into the playground.

Neat, orderly lines of pupils were marching away from the building, across the playing field and down steps into concrete bunkers. Adam had never noticed these before. Every one of the children had changed out of uniform and carried a coat and a cardboard box like Jade's.

Adam and Jade tacked themselves onto the end of one line and soon found themselves sitting, with 30 other children and a couple of teachers, on slatted wooden benches in a cold, damp dugout with a soft earth floor. The teachers, whom Adam hadn't met so far, were holding lanterns by the light of which they checked that the children were all there.

"Coats on! It's chilly down here," ordered one teacher, while the other called to Adam, "Where's your gas mask?"

"It's all right, Sir, it's here!" Jade answered for him. She thrust something onto his lap from beneath the bench. It was a cardboard box on a string, like the one she and all the others were holding.

"Well, keep it with you," said the teacher. "Don't put it down where you might lose it."

Another teacher announced, "Now remember not to ask for biscuits or water until we've been here at least half an hour. And Jade, I think it's your turn today to start the sing-song."

The children launched into a tune he didn't know (something about bluebirds over the white cliffs of Dover). Adam stared around him. He saw that one of the boys seemed to be in charge of a huge bottle of water and some paper cups, while a girl held a family-size tin of biscuits importantly on her lap. Were they intending to stay here all night? And if so, were those the only refreshments they'd get?

Adam shivered. He didn't like it down here. It smelt damp and nasty and the wooden bench was hard. "How long are we here for?" he whispered to Jade between songs.

"Until the 'All Clear', of course."

"When will that be?" asked Adam.

"Who knows?" said Jade. "Anyway, look on the bright side. We've missed the spelling test now."

Adam hadn't known there was to be a spelling test, but in any case, surely school was over for the day? He checked his watch, but found that it had stopped at quarter to four, which was the time he'd entered the cupboard.

He couldn't make sense of any of it, but as long as Jade was there he felt everything must be all right in the end. He wasn't used to the ways of this strange school yet, but Jade had been here all her life. She would look after him.

Adam was trying hard to wriggle into a more comfortable position when the droning noises he had been hearing in the air above turned into one great, deafening crash-bang. Even down here, deep in this concrete bunker, he could feel weird movements and vibrations all around. He could sense the sudden tension in the others. A couple of girls clung desperately onto each other and one of the boys began to sob until a teacher put a comforting arm around him.

What had happened? It sounded like some terrible explosion. It suddenly dawned on Adam that there was an air raid going on out there. Now he couldn't help feeling scared. He clutched at Jade's arm, but she simply grinned and said, "It's OK, that one didn't sound too close."

At last, after more thuds and bangs, plus another generous helping of sing-song, there came a long, continuous siren note which set everyone cheering. This must be the 'All Clear' that Jade had mentioned.

One of the teachers peered outside then gave the signal to go. The children filed out into the playground again, relieved and excited. It was good to move and stretch, good to warm up and return to more comfortable surroundings, even though they could see in the distance a huge fire consuming the ruins of a local factory ... a factory that Adam hadn't noticed before.

Adam was just about to panic. He didn't like what was happening to him. Was he going mad? As soon as he could he slipped away from the others and ran back into the hall. With shaking hands he thrust the iron key into the stock cupboard lock. He opened the door and flung himself in, this time securing the door on the inside.

The light went out and he waited in the dark, counting slowly up to fifty. Then he turned the key once more and stepped out into the hall, hardly daring to look.

All was well!

Immediately he cried out with relief, for everything was as it had been, before he ever entered the cupboard. The dusty, brown curtain was back in place with all the clutter piled behind it. The flowery curtains were back at the windows and the Monet artwork was up on the walls once more. Even the hands of his watch had started moving again.

Had some weird magic been at work? Or had he fallen asleep in there and dreamed it? Such a strange experience couldn't really have happened. He'd better put the key back on the teacher's desk and try to forget all about it.

He tilted his arm slightly backwards to slip the key into his pocket and felt something hanging from his shoulder. It was a cardboard box on a length of string — the box containing the gas mask Jade had given him!

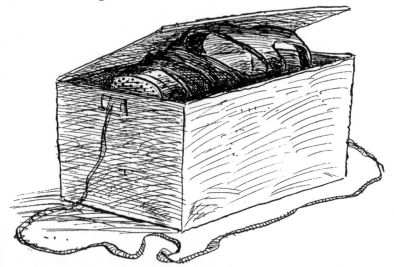

Chapter 3
Drastic Changes

Adam went back to Aunt Laura's and Uncle Tim's house where he had been staying for the last few weeks while both his parents were in hospital. Aunt Laura and Uncle Tim had been looking after him since his family had had an accident in their car. Although Adam had escaped with nothing more than a few cuts and bruises, his Dad had damaged both his legs quite seriously. Mum was said not to be too badly injured but was being kept in hospital as she was expecting a baby soon and they needed to keep an eye on her.

Uncle Tim promised that everything would be fine in the end and that Adam would belong to a proper family again. In the meantime, he would just have to be patient and try not to worry, or to mind having a different home and school for a while.

But Adam did worry. How badly were his parents hurt? No one had explained to him properly what had happened and so far he hadn't been allowed to visit them. Perhaps the unborn baby was hurt and he might never have the new brother or sister he'd been looking forward to. Besides, on a more selfish note, he certainly minded a lot that he'd had to leave behind all his friends, his familiar school, his favourite teachers and most of his gear.

Even though Adam's aunt and uncle meant to be kind they had no children of their own and were not used to having a boy in the house. They treated him like a much younger person. They kept a watchful eye on him all the time. He had to tell them whenever he went out and they sent him to bed much too early. He certainly couldn't talk things over with them or confide in them as he could in his parents. So he felt very lonely and anxious.

If it hadn't been for the gas mask, he might have blamed this anxiety for causing the strange episode in the stock cupboard. But the gas mask was real enough. He had lifted it from the box and examined it in his bedroom. He had even tried it on, disliking the closed-in, breathless feeling it gave him and its rubbery smell. How dreadful it must have been to have had to wear the thing for real!

This whole experience was a nightmare which he longed to share. But this was no time to be bothering his parents and he didn't feel Aunt Laura and Uncle Tim would understand. He guessed they would either humour him or laugh at his strange story. Even if he showed them the gas mask they might think he'd stolen it from somewhere.

The only person who might be of any help to him was Jade Green. After all, she had been mixed up in the strange experience too. He decided to hold on to the key for a while and question Jade further. She must know what was going on. Could he persuade her to go back into the stock cupboard with him?

Adam slept badly that night, but the next morning, he couldn't wait to start out for school. He knew where Jade lived and planned to walk past her house, although it was off his usual route. And suddenly there she was, back in her neat school uniform, crossing the street in front of him. Unfortunately, her friend Sophie Beale was with her. The two of them had linked arms and were chatting away together like a couple of gossipy women. Adam was too shy to interrupt.

Not until lunch time did he manage to get Jade alone. Then he showed her the key and asked if she had ever been inside the cupboard. When she said no, Adam didn't believe her. After all, she'd walked across the mystery hall with him yesterday on the way to the air-raid shelters.

"What about the secret room, then?"

Jade laughed. "Oh, that? Well, let's say it's less of a room and more of a rumour."

"All right then, what about the gas mask you gave me? Where did that come from?"

"Gas mask? I don't know what you're talking about."

"Yes, you do – I've got it here. It's hidden at the bottom of my bag. I daren't leave it behind at my aunt's in case they find it."

Now Jade stared at him with real bewilderment.

"You must have mixed me up with somebody else. I've never given you anything."

"Look, there's no need to pretend. I'm not going to get you into trouble or anything – we're in this together. I'm just trying hard to sort it all out and you're not making it any easier. If I show you the gas mask ..."

Adam began to open his bulging school bag, but Jade turned away, refusing to look.

"I don't tell lies!" she snapped, "And I certainly wouldn't give presents to people who think I do." Then with a snooty toss of her head she hurried off to find her friend Sophie.

Now Adam was really upset. If Jade would not co-operate it looked as though he would never be able to solve the mystery. He pondered his problem all through afternoon school, then finally came to a conclusion. He would give in and say nothing more to anyone. He would hide the gas mask in the stock cupboard behind a pile of books and try to forget all about it. Nothing was worth all this extra worry, especially on top of the problems he already had.

Yet he soon discovered that he was not going to be able to shrug off the mystery so easily.

Chapter 4
The Silver Monster

Next day, once again, Adam hid in the lavatories after school, then sneaked into the hall when he thought everyone except Mrs Yates had gone.

By this time he couldn't wait to get rid of the gas mask. All day it had made him feel uneasy, as if he were carrying a ticking bomb around in his bag. Even worse, every now and again a weird suspicion swept over him that he was caught up in something evil, like a wizard's magic spell.

With a rather unsteady hand he unlocked the cupboard door and stepped inside as the light came on, taking care to leave the door slightly open. First he moved a pile of exercise books from one shelf to another. Then he lifted the gas mask from his bag, pushed it into the gap he had made, then replaced the books in front of it. As he stepped backwards to judge whether the box was well enough hidden, his heel caught the edge of the door. Before he could do anything to stop it, the door slammed shut behind him, just as it had done the day before.

Adam hadn't panicked last time, knowing he had the key safely in his hand. Yet this time, although he still clutched the key, fear swept over him. The thing he had dreaded most had happened and now he couldn't ignore the problem after all. What would he find when he opened that door again?

Well, he had to open it. He couldn't stay here in the dark all night. Besides, Aunt Laura had promised to take him along to the hospital this evening to see his parents for the first time since the accident. This was a very important event, something he had waited a long time for and he didn't intend to miss it.

Adam gave the door a push in case it wasn't really locked, but it stood solid as a prison wall. He had to use the key. He stepped out in terror, hardly daring to lift his eyes.

His worst fear had come true. He was back in the mystery hall again, with its two stark posters and the blackout curtains at its taped-up windows.

Adam felt sick. He slumped to the floor and sat there with his back against the wall, not daring to move. Then suddenly, there was Jade Green again, walking towards him in her shabby dress and cardigan, though this time with no gas mask over her shoulder.

"Want to come and see the barrage balloon?" she asked. "I know it's out of bounds, but we can sneak behind the bushes round the edge of the field. They've got it on the ground today, which is something that doesn't happen often."

Adam sat there, staring foolishly. "What's going on?" he managed to croak. "I wish somebody would just tell me what's going on."

Jade laughed. "War's going on, silly! But that doesn't mean we can't have a bit of fun. Come on!"

She stretched out both arms and dragged Adam to his feet.

At least Adam was relieved to see Jade again. It meant he was no longer alone in this alien world. Surely nothing really terrible could happen if the two of them stayed together? Because he believed this, he followed her across the playground and onto the football pitch, one end of which had strangely turned itself into a vegetable garden with neat rows of cabbages, carrots and potatoes. The goalpost was gone and in its place was a huge notice saying in bold, red letters:

MINISTRY OF DEFENCE. AIR FORCE PERSONNEL ONLY BEYOND THIS POINT. TRESPASSERS WILL BE ARRESTED.

Behind the notice stretched open fields. In the farthest field Adam could already see a group of huts, with men in light blue

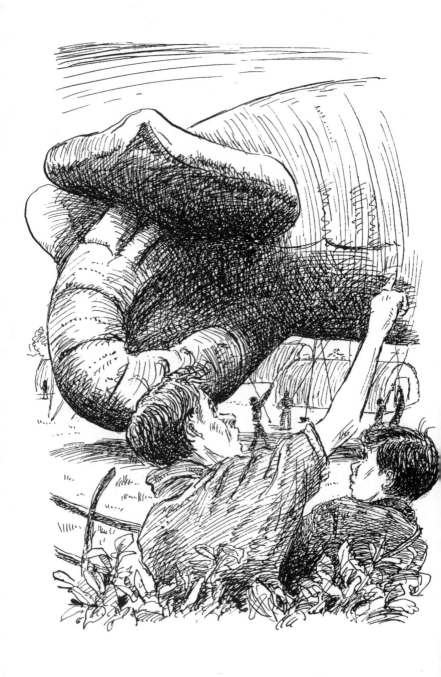

uniforms moving around a great, silver monster which seemed to be tethered to the ground.

"Look at that!" cried Jade with enthusiasm. "Isn't she a beauty? And it's our lucky day. They've taken her down for repair so we'll be able to see her properly."

"So that's a barrage balloon?" Adam had to admit it was a wonderful sight.

"What did you *think* it was? Come on, we can get much closer if we scramble through this hedge."

"But there's barbed wire."

"It's not so bad down here. We can crawl underneath it. Just keep your head down and be careful."

"But it says trespassers will be arrested."

"Only if they're caught. Anyway, that means grown-ups like German spies and such. No one's going to bother about a couple of innocent kids like us. We're finding out things. They should praise us for being interested."

Adam didn't want to lose sight of Jade, so he felt he must do as she said.

The children managed to scramble safely under the hedge. They dodged across a couple of fields. They were just creeping carefully along one side of the metal fence surrounding the balloon site when the air-raid siren sounded.

Chapter 5
Casualty!

This time they were caught in the open. Jade knew that the school's air-raid shelters were a long way off. All the same, she started to run straight across the fields towards them, not caring now whether she was spotted or not.

"Come on! We've got to get to the shelters quick!" she called to Adam.

"Can't we use those huts instead?"

"Don't be daft! They'd have our brains for breakfast!"

"You said it wouldn't matter. You said they wouldn't mind because we're only kids."

"Oh, shut up! Save your breath and follow me!"

Adam stumbled breathlessly after her. What else could he do? But he wasn't paying enough attention to where he was going. He caught his foot in a hole and fell sprawling to the ground.

Now he was really scared. He called after Jade but she didn't hear him and kept on running. Adam struggled to his feet. His ankle was hurting, but he decided it wasn't anything too serious. He was just about to move off again when the plane zoomed in.

It made a terrifying noise as it swooped low over the fields, much too low. Adam could actually see the pilot's head, in leather helmet and goggles, looking down from the cockpit. Then the plane soared upwards again and something dark came hurtling out of it.

A bomb?

There was a thunderous explosion as the missile hit the earth. A huge fountain of soil, stones, bushes and even a whole tree were flung into the air. A huge crater opened its massive jaws and the next field disappeared.

Adam had thrown himself to the ground. Something hit him on the side of the head. He heard a dreadful scream from somewhere ahead of him. He looked up in terror. He was just in time to see Jade Green's body tossed into the air before it fell like a limp rag doll into the crater and then lay still.

Chapter 6
Missing Person

Adam Belman opened his eyes. He was in a hospital bed and a nurse was bending over him.

"I think he's awake now," she was telling someone. Then she began explaining to Adam where he was.

"You're going to be fine," she told him soothingly.

Adam moved his limbs carefully one by one. Everything seemed to be in place, but he had a thumping headache and his surroundings seemed blurred.

Worst of all was the confusion. What had happened? He tried to think back, then suddenly remembered the air raid. He must have been injured in that. All at once he could see the massive crater opening in front of him and Jade Green hurtling through the air before falling into it.

He turned his head and muttered to the nurse. "Is Jade all right?"

"Jade?"

"Jade Green, the girl who was with me."

"Nobody was with you, dear, as far as I know. But your auntie's on the way, so perhaps she can sort it out for you."

As soon as Aunt Laura came in she began explaining what had happened. "Don't you remember, dear? The school caretaker accidentally locked you in the stock cupboard. She didn't know you were there, of course. When you didn't come home I rang the school and they searched around until they found you. You were unconscious. The doctor says it's nothing to worry about. You may even be having a delayed reaction from your car accident, or you may have banged your head on one of the shelves in there. There's certainly a bit of bruising behind your ear."

"I was hit by a stone or a rock," interrupted Adam, mysteriously.

"Well, never mind, dear! It's all over now. They want to keep you here for one more night for observation, then with any luck you can come home."

"She's dead, isn't she?" asked Adam.

Aunt Laura looked worried. "Nobody's dead, dear and you are going to be fine. You probably haven't realised it yet, but you are in the same hospital as your Mum and Dad. So your Mum will be coming along to see you soon and before you go home you'll be able to visit your Dad in the ward next door. Won't that be great?"

"But what about the air raid? Why will nobody talk about it?"

"Air raid?" It was clear that Aunt Laura didn't know what Adam was talking about. She was growing more and more concerned.

"It was awful, Aunt Laura! But what I really want to know is whether Jade's all right. Maybe there's a different ward for girls. Could you find out for me, please? It's very important," Adam insisted.

"Don't you worry about anybody else," Aunt Laura soothed. "You just think about getting better yourself."

In his alarm, Adam struggled to sit up. "But don't you see, I can't get better until I know what's happened to Jade? She was hurt much worse than I was."

As far as Aunt Laura knew, no one else had been involved in Adam's adventure. The boy's mind must be disturbed. However, she could see that it was important to calm him down, even if that meant pretending to go along with his story.

She consulted the nurse, then the doctor. They suggested that she ring the school to ask about this Jade person.

"He's obviously got this girl on his mind," said the doctor. "Once he realises she's all right and not involved in any way, perhaps he'll settle down."

Aunt Laura did not look very happy about this. She agreed to make the call, but in a strange way she felt almost afraid of what she might find out.

Chapter 7
Jade the Third

Aunt Laura rang the school at once, from a telephone in the corridor outside the ward. The result was that a little while later, Jade Green herself walked into the ward with Adam's uncle. Jade was carrying a huge bunch of flowers.

Adam sat up in bed, looking better already.

"You're OK, then?" he asked Jade in amazement.

At best he had imagined that she would be very badly injured.

Jade looked just as puzzled as everyone else. "I'm sorry about what happened to you," she told Adam. "I've brought you some flowers and I hope you get better soon. But I honestly don't see where I fit into all this. I'm here because your uncle told me you were worried about me being hurt, but as you can see, I'm fine."

"Don't you remember the air raid?" asked Adam.

Understanding suddenly dawned on Jade's face. "You mean the one Mr Evans was telling us about in class? Oh, I know what it is! You've been thinking about my Grandad's sister!" she said to Adam.

Jade explained to the grown-ups that she had told everyone about this great-aunt of hers during a lesson about the Second World War.

"She was called Jade Green as well. In fact, I was named after her and I'm supposed to look like she did at my age. When Mr Evans started describing the air raid that happened during the Second World War near our school, I told him that was when my great-aunt had been killed. Mr Evans asked if it would upset me to talk about it, but I said no. So I stood up in class and described what had happened, the way my Grandad has often told it to me.

"On the day of the raid, when the siren sounded, all the other children had been marched into the shelters as usual, but just before then, my Great-aunt Jade had wandered off on her own. She'd said she wanted to get a closer look at the barrage balloon which was kept in some fields behind the school."

"I know! I saw her – I was there!" insisted Adam.

"Don't be daft – you couldn't have been!" laughed Jade. "This was way back in 1942. I expect that knock on your head confused you. You got mixed up with what you'd heard in class."

"Now, that's where you're wrong!" cried Adam in triumph, "Because the gas mask was real. The one you gave me, remember? I even tried it on!"

He was determined to make everybody believe him.

Jade gave a sad little smile.

"Oh yes, I told you about the gas mask, too. My Great-aunt Jade left hers behind in school that day, something the children were told never to do. The school kept it in memory of her and as a reminder to everyone else. I believe it's still around on a shelf at the back of the stock cupboard."

Slowly, very slowly, Adam began piecing the bits of this incredible story together. He was still struggling to make some sense of it when the whole episode was driven to the back of his mind by another amazing event.

A woman had just walked into the ward carrying a small bundle wrapped in a frilly, white shawl.

"Mum!" Adam almost leapt out of bed.

Mrs Belman handed the bundle to Aunt Laura then ran to hug her son.

"Oh, Adam, it's so good to see you! And Dad's going to zoom along to visit you in his wheelchair soon. He's almost better now. He'll be walking again in a couple of weeks."

They clung onto each other as if they would never let go. But at last Mrs Belman collected her bundle from Aunt Laura and held it out to Adam.

"Meet your new little sister," she announced proudly.

Adam stared down at the tiny face and the tiny fingers clutching the edge of the shawl. And suddenly the problems and mysteries of the past, though they would never be forgotten, were gently overtaken by this wonderful new hope for the future.

"What shall we call her? Any ideas?"

"Let's call her Jade," cried Adam happily.

And that seemed to please everyone.

Who is Barrington Stoke?

Barrington Stoke was a famous and much-loved story-teller. He travelled from village to village carrying a lantern to light his way. He arrived as it grew dark and when the young boys and girls of the village saw the glow of his lantern, they hurried to the central meeting place. They were full of excitement and expectation, for his stories were always wonderful.

Then Barrington Stoke set down his lantern. In the flickering light the listeners were enthralled by his tales of adventure, horror and mystery. He knew exactly what they liked best and he loved telling a good story. And another. And then another. When the lantern burned low and dawn was nearly breaking, he slipped away. He was gone by morning, only to appear the next day in some other village to tell the next story.

Barrington Stoke would like to thank all its readers for commenting on the manuscript before publication and in particular:

Charlene Archer
Adam Boyen
Jack Bromley
Adam Burns
Charlotte Cooke
Katie Cooper
Michael Dodds
Noreen Faulkner
Sean Fitzgerald
Brendan Friendship
Nikki Gardner
Sandra Hart
Kimberley Hughes

Charlotte Impey
Kayleigh Jones
Sophie Loade
Adela Matamalas
Lucie Matamalas
Mrs A Pattinson
Lewis Roberts
Sophie Rowe
Rhona Smith
Anne Stockdale
Matthew Taylor
April Tydd
Jamie Wilson

Become a Consultant!

Would you like to give us feedback on our titles before they are published? Contact us at the email address or website below – we'd love to hear from you!

Email: info@barringtonstoke.co.uk
Website: www.barringtonstoke.co.uk

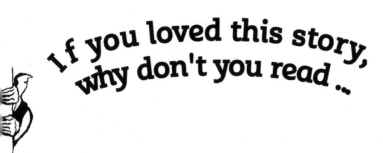

If you loved this story, why don't you read ...

Lift off !

by Hazel Townson

Have you ever wanted to miss school sports day? When Ronnie attempts to have a day at home, he certainly gets more than he bargained for when he comes face to face with an unexpected visitor.